Cheer CHOICE

BY JAKE MADDOX

text by Emma Carlson Berne
illustrated by Katie Wood

STONE ARCH BOOKS
a capstone imprint

Jake Maddox books are published by Stone Arch Books
A Capstone Imprint
1710 Roe Crest Drive
North Mankato, Minnesota 56003
www.capstonepub.com

Library of Congress Cataloging-in-Publication Data

Maddox, Jake, author.
Cheer choice / by Jake Maddox ; text by Emma Carlson Berne ;
illustrated by Katie Wood.
pages cm. ~ (Jake Maddox girl sports stories)
Summary: Colleen is devastated when her best friend changes schools~but
when she learns that Meredith is teaching her new cheerleading squad the
routine they created together for an upcoming competition their friendship
is tested.
ISBN 978-1-4342-4143-6 (hardcover) ~ ISBN 978-1-4342-7931-6 (pbk.) ~
ISBN 978-1-4342-9287-2 (eBook PDF)
1. Best friends~Juvenile fiction. 2. Cheerleading~Juvenile fiction.
3. Friendship~Juvenile fiction. 4. Decision making~Juvenile fiction.
5. Competition (Psychology)~Juvenile fiction. [1. Best friends~Fiction. 2.
Cheerleading~Fiction. 3. Friendship~Fiction. 4. Decision making~Fiction.
5. Competition (Psychology)~Fiction.] I. Berne, Emma Carlson, author. II.
Wood, Katie, 1981- illustrator. III. Title.

PZ7.M25643Ci 2014
[Fic]~dc23

2013028660

Designer: Alison Thiele
Production Specialist: Charmaine Whitman

Printed in China.
092013
007735LEOS14

TABLE OF CONTENTS

Chapter One

BIG CHANGES

"Mer! Try the toe-touch jump," Colleen called. She leaned back on her hands in the grass and squinted to see her best friend in the bright sunshine of the backyard.

Meredith leaped high in the air, bringing her legs out straight to either side and touching her toes. She landed with her feet shoulder-width apart.

"Bring your legs together more on the landing," Colleen suggested.

Meredith wiped at the sweat beading on her forehead. "Okay," she said.

Colleen watched as Meredith bent her knees and launched herself even higher into the air. She flung her feet out to the sides and pointed her toes before snapping her legs together sharply as she landed.

"That was perfect!" Colleen cried, leaping to her feet. "Let's try it together."

Colleen positioned herself next to her friend and placed her hands on her hips. Both girls stared straight ahead, feet wide apart as they got ready to run through their cheerleading routine.

"Ready? Go!" Meredith shouted.

They both jumped high for the toe touch before landing and moving immediately into a back handspring.

Colleen concentrated on moving her body in rhythm with Meredith's. Together, they dropped to one knee.

"And this is where we do the basket toss with a twist," Meredith said.

They each mimed a basket toss, since they didn't have the rest of the squad. They followed that with a cartwheel, then moved directly into splits.

"Now the spin and arabesque," Meredith continued. "And then dismount . . ."

The two girls spaced out and flung themselves into front handsprings, finishing with a roundoff, their arms high in the air.

"Perfect!" Meredith said.

Colleen turned and gave her friend a high five. "That was awesome!" she said. "This is seriously the best routine ever."

Meredith nodded. The two collapsed onto the grass to catch their breath.

"I can't believe how long we've been working on this routine," Colleen said. "It's taken all summer!"

"Three months," Meredith agreed quietly, looking down at the grass.

"I can't wait until we present it to the rest of the squad," Colleen said with a grin. "The two co-captains with the newest, coolest routine."

But instead of smiling, Meredith just twirled a blade of grass between her fingers. "I need to tell you something," she said quietly. Meredith's voice was so low that Colleen had to lean forward to hear her friend.

"What's the matter?" Colleen asked.

"I'm moving," Meredith said. She finally looked up, and Colleen saw that her friend had tears in her eyes.

For a long minute, Colleen just stared at Meredith. "What do you mean you're moving?" she asked. "Where?"

"We're moving to Fenton," Meredith said, choking up a little. "My parents told me last week. I'll be going to Fenton Public."

Colleen couldn't believe it. "You're going to another school?" she said. "But what about the cheer squad? What about being co-captains?"

Colleen's throat was thick with tears. She couldn't imagine not seeing her best friend every day. And even worse, not cheering with her.

Meredith put her arm around Colleen's shoulders. "Well . . . we won't be able to be captains together anymore. But we'll always be best friends," she said.

Colleen nodded and hugged Meredith as she tried to fight back tears. Even though she wanted to believe her friend's words, she had a feeling that a lot was about to change.

Chapter Two

BREAKING THE NEWS

The following afternoon, Colleen stood outside the cheerleading coach's office. After Meredith had left, Coach Ryan had called and asked Colleen to come in for a meeting before the squad's first practice.

Colleen took a deep breath and knocked softly on the door, pushing it open a crack.

Coach Ryan looked up from her computer and smiled. "Come on in, Colleen," she said.

Colleen walked in and sat down in front of the coach's desk. For the millionth time, she swiped at her swollen eyes. She felt like she'd been crying since Meredith had told her the news.

"Well, Meredith's parents came in to see me a couple days ago," the coach began. She smiled at Colleen sympathetically. "They told me they're moving. We're all really going to miss Meredith."

The tears threatened to spill over again, but Colleen fought them back. "Yeah," she whispered. She didn't trust her voice to speak any louder than that.

"Of course, since you and Meredith were co-captains, this leaves us with the problem of leading the squad," Coach Ryan continued.

Colleen nodded. "I know," she said quietly.

The coach glanced down at a piece of paper in front of her. "I don't think the squad is ready for a big change this close to the All-Stars Competition," she said. "Do you think you can captain the squad by yourself?"

Colleen swallowed. She couldn't imagine leading the cheers without Meredith, especially at the All-Stars Competition! It was the biggest annual cheerleading event in their district.

But I don't want anyone to take Meredith's place, Colleen thought. *I guess it's better to just do it alone.*

Colleen nodded. "Yeah, I can do it," she told the coach.

"I know you can," Coach Ryan agreed with a smile. "I'm proud of you, Colleen. And I know the squad will appreciate you stepping up too."

The coach pushed back her chair and stood up. "The rest of the squad is already waiting in the gym," she said. "Why don't you head in and explain what's happening? I'll need to finish up a few things, and I'll meet you there."

Slowly, Colleen made her way out to the gym. She didn't want to face the rest of the squad. No one was going to be happy that Meredith was gone.

The other cheerleaders were all sitting on the gym floor, chatting and stretching when Colleen came in. She walked to stand in front of them, and everyone fell silent.

It felt strange standing there alone. Colleen was used to having her co-captain by her side. For a long moment, she couldn't think of what to say.

Then, Dani, a tall girl with a long, dark braid, broke the silence. "What's up, Colleen?" she called out. "Where's Meredith?"

Colleen took a deep breath. *I just have to tell them and get it over with*, she thought.

"I have some bad news, guys," she started. "Meredith is moving. She's leaving the squad and going to Fenton."

Several of the girls gasped. The entire squad looked upset.

"What are we going to do?" Andrea, a freshman, asked. "What about the All-Stars Competition?"

Colleen looked at the worried faces all around her. *The squad is depending on me*, she thought. *I'm the only captain now, and I have to act that way.*

Colleen took a deep breath. "We're going to be just fine," she said. Her voice sounded way more confident than she actually felt. "And I'm not going anywhere, so don't worry. I'll just be a solo captain instead of a co-captain."

The girls relaxed. A few of them even smiled.

Colleen forced herself to smile back at everyone. "Come on, everyone, huddle up," she said.

Everyone huddled close and put their hands together in the middle of the circle.

"On three!" Colleen shouted.

"One, two, three, cheer!" the squad shouted together, flinging their hands high in the air.

Colleen made sure she shouted as loud as the rest of the girls. They were depending on her now. And no one could know just how sad and worried she really was.

Chapter Three

AN UNWELCOME SURPRISE

Later that week, Colleen sat in the passenger seat of her mom's car. They were parked outside Fenton Public, Meredith's new school.

Her mother glanced over at her from the driver's seat. "Are you nervous about visiting Meredith?" Mom asked.

Colleen glanced at the gymnasium. Even from the parking lot, she could hear the shouts and the squeaking of sneakers.

"Of course not," Colleen said, trying to squash the butterflies in her stomach. "Why would I be nervous?"

Mom gave her a knowing look. "Just checking, sweetie," she said. "I'll come back and pick you up in half an hour or so, okay?"

Colleen nodded as she grabbed her backpack and jumped out of the car. When Meredith had asked her to come see her practice with her new cheer team, Colleen had been so excited to see her friend she'd agreed. But now she was feeling more scared than excited.

What if it's weird seeing Meredith cheering with a new squad? Colleen worried. *What if she decided she doesn't really want me hanging around after all?*

Still, she couldn't stand in the parking lot all afternoon. Colleen tugged open the gym doors and went inside. The Fenton cheer squad was at the far end of the gym. All the girls stood in a line with their hands on their hips and feet apart. They were obviously just about to start a routine.

Colleen took a seat on the bleachers and balanced her backpack in her lap. It was easy to spot Meredith in the middle of the line. Meredith hadn't seen her yet, but Colleen wasn't worried.

We can talk during a break, Colleen thought, leaning back on the bleachers to watch the team practice. *I'm glad I came after all.*

"Ready? Let's go!" Meredith shouted to the squad.

The girls brought their hands together with a loud clap and then jumped into a toe-touch split. They repeated the move three times. Then they spread out across the tumbling mats to do their back handsprings.

The cheerleaders quickly recovered and formed four clusters. They raised the flyers up off the ground. Crouching down slightly, the girls at the bases tossed the flyers into the air. The flyers revolved like spinning sticks before landing.

Colleen gasped. Toe-touch split three times, back handspring, basket toss with a twist . . .

This is the routine Meredith and I came up with, Colleen realized in disbelief. *Meredith taught it to her new squad.*

Colleen's heart was pounding as she watched the squad move through the rest of the routine. It was exactly the same, move for move.

"Great job, guys!" Meredith shouted when they were done.

"Let's take five and get some water," the coach called from her seat.

Meredith spotted Colleen on the bench and ran toward her. "Colleen! You came!" she called, smiling happily.

Colleen felt her face flush. *How could she teach them our special routine?* she thought furiously. *It was supposed to be for us!*

Meredith hugged Colleen. "I've missed you so much!" she squealed. Then she pulled back and studied her friend's face. "Hey, what's wrong?"

"I can't believe you're using our routine with your new squad," Colleen said. "We came up with that together." She felt tears gathering under her eyelids.

Meredith looked confused. "I don't get it," she said, shaking her head. "I taught it to them because it's the best one I know. We're going to do it at the All-Stars Competition. I didn't know it was just for us and the old team."

"Well, we made it up together," Colleen said. "But obviously, you've forgotten all about that. And everything else about your old life, including your old squad and your old friends."

I can't believe Meredith doesn't even seem sorry! Colleen thought. Her tears had disappeared, and anger had taken over.

Meredith's cheeks were bright red. "That routine is just as much mine as it is yours," she said, crossing her arms in front of her chest. "And I can teach it to anyone I want."

Colleen grabbed her backpack from the bleachers. "Actually, you can't," she snapped at Meredith. "That routine was created for my squad. That means we should be the ones to use it. After all, you're the one who left."

"You don't own the routine!" Meredith hollered, glaring at Colleen.

Just then, Meredith's new coach came hurrying over to them. "Girls!" she interrupted, looking between them. "What's all the yelling about? Anything I can help with?"

Colleen shook head. "Nothing's wrong," she replied, still looking at Meredith. "Nothing except people who've forgotten everything they left behind."

Colleen turned and marched out the door, leaving Meredith staring after her.

Chapter Four

SAME OLD, SAME OLD

Colleen stared out the window silently
during the car ride back. As soon as her
mother pulled up in front of her own
school, Colleen jumped out. She was late for
practice.

Coach Ryan and the rest of the squad
were already in the gym when Colleen
hurried inside. Coach Ryan glanced up
from her clipboard as Colleen took a seat
on the floor with the other girls.

"Oh, good, you're here, Colleen," Coach Ryan said. "I was just reminding everyone about the All-Stars Competition next week. The squads from all the local school districts will be there."

Colleen nodded. Even after her fight with Meredith, it was impossible to forget about the competition.

"Why don't you girls get warmed up and start running through the routine?" Coach Ryan continued. "I have to finish a few things, and then I'll check in."

Coach Ryan left the gym, and the rest of the squad turned to Colleen. She pushed away all the rotten feelings from earlier and forced herself to focus on the practice.

"Okay, guys!" Colleen said, clapping her hands. "Positions!"

The girls jumped to their feet and formed a triangle facing the bleachers. Everyone stood in start position with their hands on their hips and their feet together.

"Ready? Go!" Colleen shouted from her place at the top of the triangle.

Everyone jumped their legs apart and put their arms in the air before performing a somersault followed by a cartwheel. Then they spread out to do a high split-leg jump.

Colleen could tell she wasn't jumping as high as normal, but she couldn't help it. She didn't have much energy today.

The girls moved into three groups. The bases all gathered around their flyers, who stood straight with their arms in the air. The bases tossed the flyers high, caught them, and finished on one knee.

The squad had been working on their routine for the All-Stars Competition for months. It was a good, solid routine. Sometimes Colleen felt like she could do it in her sleep.

It might put the judges to sleep too, Colleen thought. *It's kind of boring. But I can't tell the other girls that.*

Colleen turned to the others, panting a little. "Nice job, guys!" she said, trying to sound enthusiastic. "That's the way we'll take it to All-Stars."

The rest of the team glanced at each other. Then Dani spoke up. "Listen, Colleen," she said. "A few of us were talking before practice, and to be honest, we don't think this routine can win at All-Stars, no matter how well we do it."

"It's not cool enough," Anna called from the back of the group. "We need more spice!"

There were murmurs of agreement and nods from the rest of the squad.

Colleen sighed. "Honestly, guys, I agree with you," she said. "But what other choice do we have? All-Stars is a week away. And we already know this routine. I think we just have to go with it."

"What about that new routine you were working on with Meredith?" Dani suggested. "You guys said you were going to show it to us, but you never did."

Colleen pursed her lips. The new routine was probably good enough to win. But . . .

"I don't think there's enough time to learn it," she said.

"Oh, come on!" Anna chimed in. "We'll really practice. We can learn it in a week. You said it's awesome, right?"

Colleen nodded slowly. It was awesome. But Meredith's squad would be using it at the All-Stars Competition too.

Are we really going to use our own routine against each other? Colleen thought.

Chapter Five

THE RIGHT DECISION?

Colleen could hardly sleep that night.
Her mind kept racing. She couldn't stop
thinking about her fight with Meredith and
the nervous faces of her squad. She had to
make a decision about the new routine.

Finally, Colleen shoved back her covers
and climbed out of bed. The room was hot
and stuffy. She opened a window and let
cool air in, hoping it would help her clear
her mind.

No matter how mad she was at Meredith, Colleen knew she couldn't make a decision without talking to her.

Colleen grabbed her cell phone. Meredith always slept with her phone next to her bed, and she always woke up when it buzzed.

I need to talk to you. Call me, Colleen texted, her heart pounding

She waited a few minutes, but there was no reply.

Mer, this is really important, Colleen wrote. *Seriously. Call me!*

Still nothing.

I can't believe she's ignoring me! Colleen thought angrily. *She doesn't even want to talk.*

Colleen stared at her phone for a few minutes, trying to make up her mind.

Fine, she finally decided. *If that's how Meredith wants to act, why should I care what she thinks? I'll show the squad the new routine tomorrow. Forget Meredith. She's obviously forgotten me.*

Still, even with her mind made up, it was a long time before Colleen could fall asleep.

* * *

Colleen's feet felt heavy the next afternoon as she walked to the gym after school. Even though she'd decided to use the new routine, she wasn't looking forward to using it against her best friend.

Former best friend, Colleen reminded herself, thinking of the unanswered texts. *Meredith doesn't care, so why should I?*

Coach Ryan was sitting in a folding chair in the corner of the gym, looking over diagrams. She looked up and smiled as Colleen walked over.

"Are you girls all set for practice today?" the coach asked. "The routine for All-Stars is looking pretty solid, right?"

Colleen nodded and swallowed hard. "Yeah," she said. "I might show them a few new things too."

Coach Ryan nodded. "Great!" she said. "I'm sure whatever you have will be fantastic." She smiled at Colleen reassuringly.

When the squad was all there, Colleen took a deep breath. She knew she just had to get it over with. It was now or never for the new routine.

"Okay, listen up, everyone!" Colleen shouted. "Dani was right. Our old routine for All-Stars is a little boring. So let's shake things up a bit! I'm going to show you the new routine Meredith and I created. I think it's just what we need to take home the trophy next week."

Everyone cheered and started chattering excitedly. Before she could change her mind, Colleen started demonstrating the routine. She mimed the basket toss with the spinning throw, followed by an arabesque.

Everyone cheered enthusiastically when she was finished. Colleen smiled. The new routine was much better than their other one.

"That looks awesome!" Anna shouted. "Let's try it out."

But as Colleen watched the squad run through the new routine, she felt sad. *I made the only decision I could,* she thought. *So why don't I feel happier?*

Chapter Six

DOING THE RIGHT THING

The next week seemed to drag. Every day, Colleen trudged to class. And every afternoon, she trudged to cheerleading practice.

The new routine was coming together really well. Every day, the bases got more solid, and the flyers were able to lift their legs higher in the arabesque. Everyone's split-leg jumps were higher and their legs were straighter.

The entire squad was pumped up about showing off their new routine at All-Stars. Everyone except Colleen.

On the Wednesday before the competition, the squad gathered in the gym to run through the routine again. All the cheerleaders got into position in the triangle as they practiced back handsprings.

Colleen stood at the point of the triangle and flung herself over backward with the rest of the girls, but she wasn't really paying attention. She couldn't stop thinking about how Meredith would react when she saw what Colleen and the squad had planned for All-Stars.

Suddenly, Colleen realized the music had stopped. She glanced up and looked around in confusion.

Dani was standing next to the MP3 player and speakers. She looked irritated. "Colleen!" she said. "What is the matter with you? You're moving in slow motion."

Colleen's mouth fell open. She glanced around at the rest of the squad. Everyone else looked upset too.

Dani kept talking. "You've been acting totally out of it ever since we decided on the new routine," she continued. "It's like you're not even awake half the time. How are we supposed to win at All-Stars if we have a captain who's barely paying attention?"

Colleen felt her face grow hot with embarrassment. *Dani's right,* she thought. *The squad is depending on me. I can't let my problems get in the way. I have to find a way to fix things.*

Just then, Coach Ryan stuck her head out of the office. "What's going on?" the coach asked the squad. "I heard the music stop. Did you girls run through the basket toss already?"

Colleen stepped forward. "Everything's fine, Coach Ryan," she said. Her voice echoed in the gym. "But could I talk to you for a second?"

Coach Ryan looked surprised. She stepped back and motioned for Colleen to come into her office. She turned to the rest of the squad. "Why don't you girls take a quick water break?" she said.

Colleen closed the door behind her. "Coach, I need to talk to you about something pretty serious," she said. "It's about the routine."

"It's looking great!" the coach interrupted. "I can't wait for you girls to show it off on Sunday."

Colleen shifted nervously in her seat. "Actually . . ." she said. "There's something you don't know about the routine."

Briefly, she explained what had happened — how she and Meredith had created the routine, their fight at Meredith's new school, and Colleen's decision to use the routine at All-Stars.

"And now I don't know what to do," Colleen said. "This just doesn't feel right."

Coach Ryan nodded slowly. "This is a hard situation, Colleen," she said. "There's nothing wrong with using the same routine as Meredith's squad. It's not against the rules or anything."

"I just don't know," Colleen said. "I'm so mad at Meredith, but if I use the routine too, she'll be even madder at me. But if I don't use it, the squad will be mad."

"You have to decide what you think is right, Colleen," her coach said. "I just want you to consider one thing. How are you going to feel about yourself if you use that routine in competition? I think once you answer that question, you'll know what to do."

Coach Ryan pushed back her chair, and they both stood up. As Colleen walked out of the office, she thought hard about what her coach had said.

I know how I'll feel about myself if we use the new routine at All-Stars, she realized. *The same way I've been feeling all week — terrible*

Colleen made her way outside. She walked around the soccer field, thinking hard. By the time she got back to the gym, she knew what she had to do.

Colleen had butterflies in her stomach as she took her place in front of the rest of the squad. She took a deep breath and made herself speak firmly and clearly — like a captain should.

"Girls, we're going to have to make some changes," Colleen said. "We can't do the new routine at All-Stars. I haven't been totally honest with you."

"What do you mean?" Dani asked.

"Meredith's squad is doing that routine," Colleen said. "It wouldn't be right for us to do it too. We'll have to just stick with our old routine. I'm sorry."

Colleen felt a wave of relief as she spoke. The rest of the squad gasped and chattered to each other.

The squad might be mad at her. They most likely wouldn't win at All-Stars. And Meredith might still be using their routine.

But at least I know I'm doing the right thing, Colleen thought.

Chapter Seven

ALL-STARS

The day of the All-Stars Competition, Colleen and the rest of the squad met at the school. They all took a bus to the convention center together.

Colleen glanced around as she entered the building. It was packed with different squads, and everyone was busy warming up for the competition. The bleachers were already filling up with parents who had come to watch.

Coach Ryan gestured the squad over to an empty corner. Everyone started pulling off their warm-ups and putting on their clean competition sneakers.

Colleen laced up her own shoes and bent over to touch her toes a few times, trying to loosen up her hamstrings. The competition would start in just a few minutes.

Colleen glanced around a few times, trying to spot Meredith, but it was no use. The place was a zoo. She didn't see her friend anywhere.

Doesn't matter, Colleen told herself. *Meredith probably doesn't want to see me anyway.*

"Everyone, stay loose, and make sure to keep drinking water," Colleen called to her squad.

Colleen unscrewed her own water bottle and sighed. She'd forgotten to fill it this morning. "I'll be back in a second, guys," she said.

Colleen made her way across the gym to the water fountain. She was almost there when she ran into another girl.

"Oh, sorry," Colleen started to say as she glanced up. Then she recognized her best friend's face. "Meredith!"

"Oh, Colleen!" Meredith exclaimed, grabbing Colleen's shoulders. "I knew you'd be here! Are you mad at me? I lost my phone the other day! I just found it this morning and saw all your texts. What did you want to talk to me about?"

Colleen started to reply, but Meredith kept talking.

"I feel so bad about our fight the other day," Meredith said. "I never should have yelled at you like that. I'm so sorry! I've felt so terrible ever since, I can hardly concentrate."

"Me too!" Colleen exclaimed. "The squad basically told me I was acting like a zombie. Mer, I'm so sorry. I don't know how everything got so out of control. The routine we —"

"I know," Meredith interrupted. "There's something I have to tell you something about that too —"

But just then, Meredith's coach shouted to her from across the gym, breaking up their conversation. "Meredith, we need you for the run-through!" she hollered. "We're up first!"

"Shoot, I have to go! I'll talk to you after?" Meredith called over her shoulder as she hurried away.

"Definitely!" Colleen called back with a smile.

Colleen watched as Meredith rejoined her new squad. She felt so much better after talking to her friend.

Meredith took her position in the middle of the line of cheerleaders. "Ready? Let's go!" she shouted.

The squad clapped their hands, then formed clusters for a half-lift. The flyers' feet rested on the thighs of the bases. They held the position for a few seconds, then dropped down and ran to opposite sides of the mat before cartwheeling back across in opposing lines.

Wait a minute, Colleen thought as she watched. *This doesn't look anything like our routine. It's totally different.*

The girls on Meredith's squad dropped into half-splits with their arms raised in the air, then leaped into pikes. They ran into positions, and the bases lifted the flyers into a split for the final stunt.

Colleen ran over as soon as the flyers dropped down and the run-through of the routine was finished.

"Meredith!" she cried. "You . . . you're not —" She couldn't even get the words out.

"We're not performing our routine," Meredith said, grinning at Colleen. "You were right. We came up with that routine together. Unless we can do it together, I don't want to do it at all."

Colleen grabbed her friend into a huge hug. She was so grateful she hadn't used the routine. And so grateful to have her best friend back.

"I feel exactly the same way," Colleen agreed.

Chapter Eight

A FRIENDSHIP FIXED

"Fourth place is a strong finish," Coach Ryan told the squad as the competition drew to a close. "I'm really proud of you girls."

Out on the floor, the other squads were packing up to leave. Colleen looked across the gym and saw Meredith's squad standing around their own coach. The squad had been disqualified when two of the cheerleaders stepped off the mat.

"We did our best," Colleen chimed in. "Your somersaults were awesome, Dani."

Dani nodded. She seemed to be thinking about something else. Then Colleen saw her whisper to Anna, who nodded eagerly.

"Hang on, you guys, okay?" Dani said. She grabbed Anna's arm, and the two girls ran off.

Colleen saw her whisper to one of the judges, who thought for a moment, then nodded. Dani and Anna disappeared into the crowd for a moment. When they reappeared, they were pulling Meredith by the hand.

As soon as they reached the squad, the girls surrounded Meredith. They all hugged their old teammate. Everyone started talking at once.

"What's going on?" Colleen asked. "What are you guys up to?"

"We can't leave without showing our best routine — even if it won't count for the competition," Dani said. "We can do it just for fun. And I know exactly which routine we should do. The one our co-captains created."

"Yes!" everyone yelled together.

Meredith and Colleen grinned. They were finally going to perform their routine, just like they'd wanted all along.

The people still in the gym looked up in surprise as the squad ran to the front. Colleen didn't care that most of the people who'd come to watch were gone.

I just want to cheer with my best friend, she thought happily.

The squad arranged themselves in a triangle, and the music began. All at once, the girls flung themselves into the three starting jumps.

Colleen heard her feet hit the mat at the same time as Meredith's. As one unit, the girls lifted their arms in the air and dropped to one knee.

Even if we can't cheer together forever, at least we can right now, Colleen thought as they finished the routine. *And that feels pretty great.*

Author Bio

Emma Carlson Berne has written more than a dozen books for children and young adults, including teen romance novels, biographies, and history books. She lives in Cincinnati, Ohio, with her husband, Aaron, her son, Henry, and her dog, Holly.

Illustrator Bio

Katie Wood fell in love with drawing when she was very small. Since graduating from Loughborough University School of Art and Design in 2004, she has been living her dream working as a freelance illustrator. From her studio in Leicester, England, she creates bright and lively illustrations for books and magazines all over the world.

Glossary

annual (AN-yoo-uhl) — happening once every year

competition (kom-puh-TISH-uhn) — a contest of some kind

confident (KON-fuh-duhnt) — having a strong belief in your own abilities

disbelief (diss-bi-LEEF) — refusal to believe something

enthusiastic (en-thoo-zee-ASS-tik) — very excited or interested in something

rhythm (RITH-uhm) — a regular beat in music, poetry, or dance

routine (roo-TEEN) — a regular way or pattern of doing things

squad (SKWAHD) — a small group of people involved in the same activity, such as soldiers, football players, or police officers

Discussion Questions

1. Talk about how the relationship between Colleen and Meredith changed from the beginning of this story to the end.

2. Do you think Meredith was right to teach her new squad the routine she and Colleen created? Talk about your opinion.

3. Did Colleen make the right choice when it came to not performing the new routine at the competition? Talk about what you would have done if you were in Colleen's position.

Writing Prompts

1. Have you and a friend ever had an argument when it comes to sports or something else? Write about what happened and how you resolved things.

2. Colleen is sad when she finds out her best friend is moving away. Have you ever had a friend move? Write about how you felt and what you did to keep in touch.

3. Pretend you are Colleen's cheerleading coach. Write a paragraph about the advice you would have given her.

More about Cheerleading

Cheerleading involves many different moves and stunts. These can be done individually or combined to create a full cheerleading routine. Want to learn more about some of the moves in this book? Check them out below.

arabesque — a flyer points her leg out behind her body and turns her hip socket out so when the leg is out straight, the front of the leg is facing the audience and her arms are in a "T" position.

basket toss — the bases throw a flyer up in the air, where she then extends her legs out to the side and reaches for her toes. The flyer lands back in a cradle position created by the bases' arms.

handspring — an acrobatic move in which a person lunges headfirst from an upright position into a handstand. She then pushes off from the floor with her hands, flipping her body over and landing back in an upright position.

roundoff — a move similar to a cartwheel that turns horizontal speed into vertical speed, letting a cheerleader jump higher. A roundoff also turns forward momentum from a run into backwards momentum, giving speed and power to backwards moves such as flips and somersaults.

toe-touch — keeping her head and chest up, a cheerleader jumps in the air and reaches her legs into splits position. She makes sure to reach for her heels rather than her toes. This gives the illusion that her legs are inverted or hyperextended.